BARNYARD
SLAM

by
Dian Curtis
Regan

illustrated by
Paul
Meisel

Holiday House / New York

For Lane and Lake Potts   —D. C. R.

For my Dad (who, thanks to a "part"
from the barnyard—a bovine valve—
is still around slammin')   —P. M.

Text copyright © 2009 by Dian Curtis Regan
Illustrations copyright © 2009 by Paul Meisel
All Rights Reserved
HOLIDAY HOUSE is registered in the U.S. Patent and Trademark Office.
Printed and Bound in Malaysia
The text typeface is Aunt Mildred.
The artwork for this book was made with pencil and watercolor
on watercolor paper.
www.holidayhouse.com
First Edition
1 3 5 7 9 10 8 6 4 2
Library of Congress Cataloging-in-Publication Data
Regan, Dian Curtis.
Barnyard slam / by Dian Curtis Regan ; illustrated by Paul Meisel.—1st ed.
p. cm.
Summary: Farm animals express themselves at a poetry slam
hosted by Yo Mama Goose.
ISBN-13: 978-0-8234-1907-4
[1. Poetry slams—Fiction. 2. Domestic animals—Fiction.
3. Humorous stories.] I. Meisel, Paul, ill. II. Title.
P7.R25854Bar 2006
[E]—dc22
2005050293

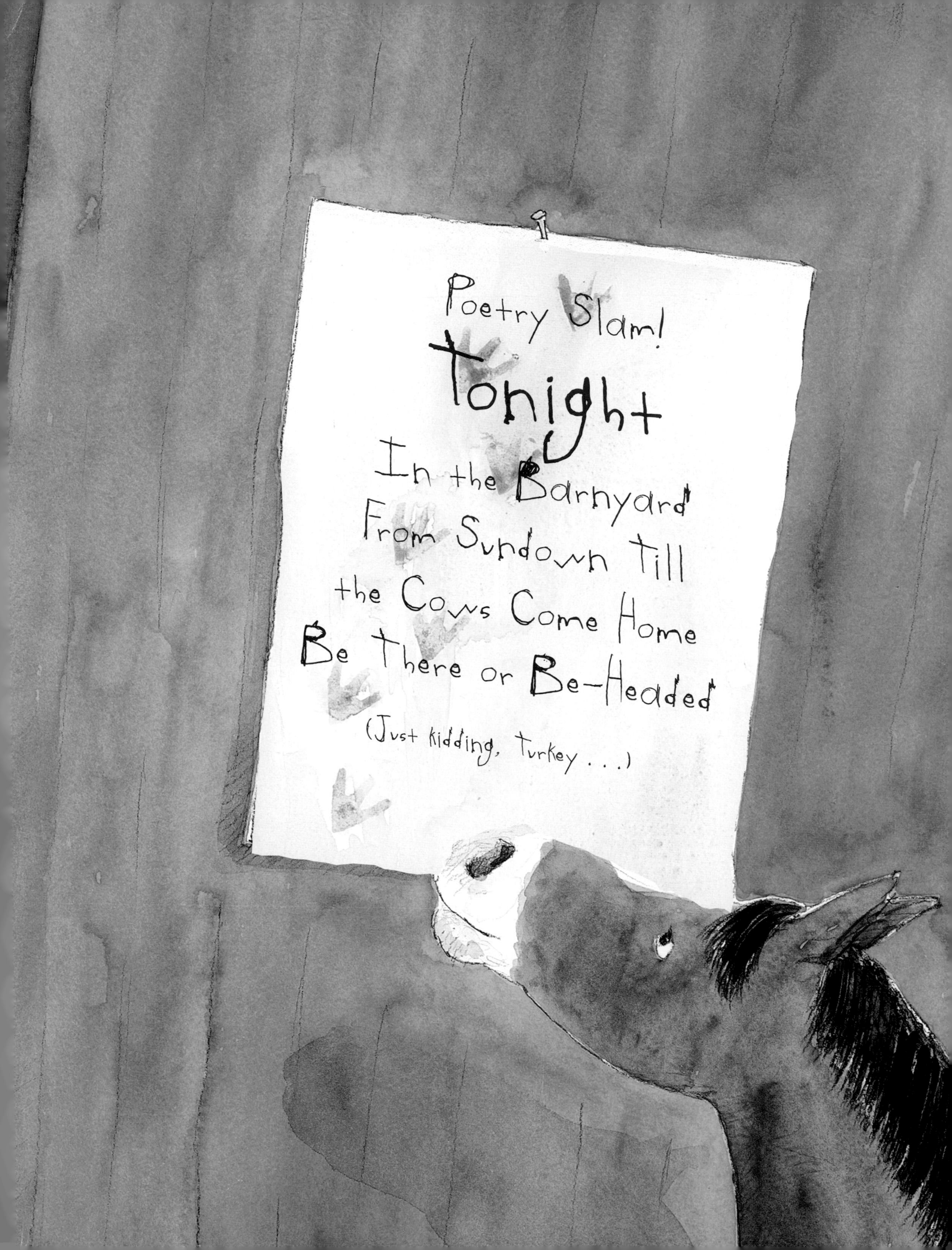
Poetry Slam!
Tonight
In the Barnyard
From Sundown till
the Cows Come Home
Be There or Be-Headed
(Just kidding, turkey . . .)

"Good evening, animals and poultry.
I am your hostess, Yo Mama Goose."

"House Mouse, please stand guard and warn us
if Farmer and Son head toward the barnyard."

"Yes, Yo."

"It's Yo *Mama*," Goose snipes.

"First up,
    performing her stunning poetry,
    please welcome . . . me!
    Behold the graceful goose
    in flight—"

"Stop!"

"Duck, what is it?"

"You cannot go first.
    The hostess
    always performs *last.*"

"I don't like being last,"
    Goose grumbles,
"and I don't like ducks.
    What a bunch of quacks."

Charley Horse limps
onto the stage.
"Well, if no one is going
to introduce me,
I will simply begin.
My poem is titled . . . **Hay!**

Yesterday–hay.
Today–hay.
Every day–hay!
Neigh, neigh, neigh!
I am sick of hay.
It is tasteless and it's scratchy.
Too much fiber!
Too much fiber!
Keeps me always on the go.
Look, it's time for dinner.
Can you guess what's
on the menu?"

"What's that? Oats? Tonight?
No hay today?
Never mind."

"Thank you, Charley Horse," says Yo Mama Goose.
"Hope that leg cramp of yours is better.
Next, audience, give it up for Cow!"

"My stage name," Cow scoffs, "is *Bovina*.
And my poem is titled
The Truth about Cows.

We have had enough of reading
all the lies, and we are needing
to correct the record
and to set it straight.
This, my friends, has **never** been our fate:

Cows do not jump over the moon.
We do not know a dish or spoon—
or why they ran away. Who cares?

We do not sit in fields of flowers,
sniffing daisies by the hours.
BULL-oney!

We do not dance.
It's all just hype.
We do not sing.
We do not type.

And to that poet who insists
that purple cattle must exist—
I. Say. This. . . .
Hogwash!"

"Hogwash?" Hog cries,
bumping Cow off the stage.
"That's the title of *my* poem,
and it goes like this:

Hogwash!
What exactly does it mean?
Do you think that we're not clean?
We bathe a lot:
We roll in mud; we roll in slime.
We roll in sand; we roll in grime.
Ahhhhh, heavenly, heavenly baths!
Hogwash!"

"Wild, Hog!" cheers Goose.
"Now quit hogging the stage.
The audience is waiting
on all fours for my performance."

"Noooooo!" cries Duck.
"Introduce me first—
the most famous duck
in the barnyard!"

"More like the most *lamest* duck,"
Goose mumbles.
"I have a program to follow.
I cannot change horses
in midstream."

"Did someone call me?"
Charley Horse asks.
"Did my poem win?"

"Hold your horses, Charley.
I'm ready for my close-up,"
Duck calls.

"Okay, audience," Goose says.
"Let's see how lucky Duck is."

"My poem is titled
Daily Decisions of a Duck.

*Do I waddle on the bank
or dive into the water?
Every day, I must decide
one or the AW-dur.*"

"Did someone call me?"
Charley Horse asks.
"Did my poem win?"

"Hold your horses, Charley.
I'm ready for my close-up,"
Duck calls.

"Okay, audience," Goose says.
"Let's see how lucky Duck is."

"My poem is titled
Daily Decisions of a Duck.

Do I waddle on the bank
or dive into the water?
Every day, I must decide
one or the AW-dur."

"Is *that* supposed to rhyme?"
  sneers Goose.

"It *did* rhyme.
  I made it rhyme."

"Whatever,"
  Goose groans.
"Give my regards
  to Fraud-way."

"My turn! My turn!"
cries Lamb, making a beeline
to the stage.

"My poem is titled **Lamb I Am**.

I would not leave my friendly flocks.
I would not follow Wolf or Fox.
I do not trust them.
Lamb I am.

I would not meet them on a trip.
I could not greet them on a ship.
I do not trust them here or there.
I do not trust them anywhere.
Lamb I am."

"Excellent!" Goose beams. "I heard it straight from the horse's mouth that Lamb wrote his poem in only two shakes of his tail."

"Well, *I* thought Lamb chopped." Duck sniffs. "Can we please stop horsing around?"

"Did someone call me?" asks Charley Horse. "Did my poem win?"

"Noooooooo!" chorus the animals.

Goose takes the stage.
"Next, please welcome . . . Turkey!"

"I wrote a gobblely-good poem,
but I do not think your sign,
Be There or Be-Headed, is funny.
It stopped me cold turkey.
Quite an insult to poultry everywhere.
I refuse to perform."

"Well," says Yo Mama Goose.
"This leaves a gaping hole in our program.
I guess *I'll* have to fill in for Turkey.
Behold the graceful goo—"

"Stop!" cries Duck. "Get off the stage
before this turns into a wild goose chase."

"Stop badgering me."

"Don't bring Badger into this."

"Okay then. Rooster, put away your comb.
You're up next."

"Wait!" cries House Mouse.
"Farmer and Son are on their way."

"Mouse, you'd better not be crying wolf."

"Wolf?" shrieks Lamb.

"Don't have a cow, Lamb.

Everybody act normal!"

"Behold the graceful goose in flight.
Winging silent through the night.
Feathers glow by light of moon.
Fly south in winter, north in June."

"Who ruffled Goose's feathers?"

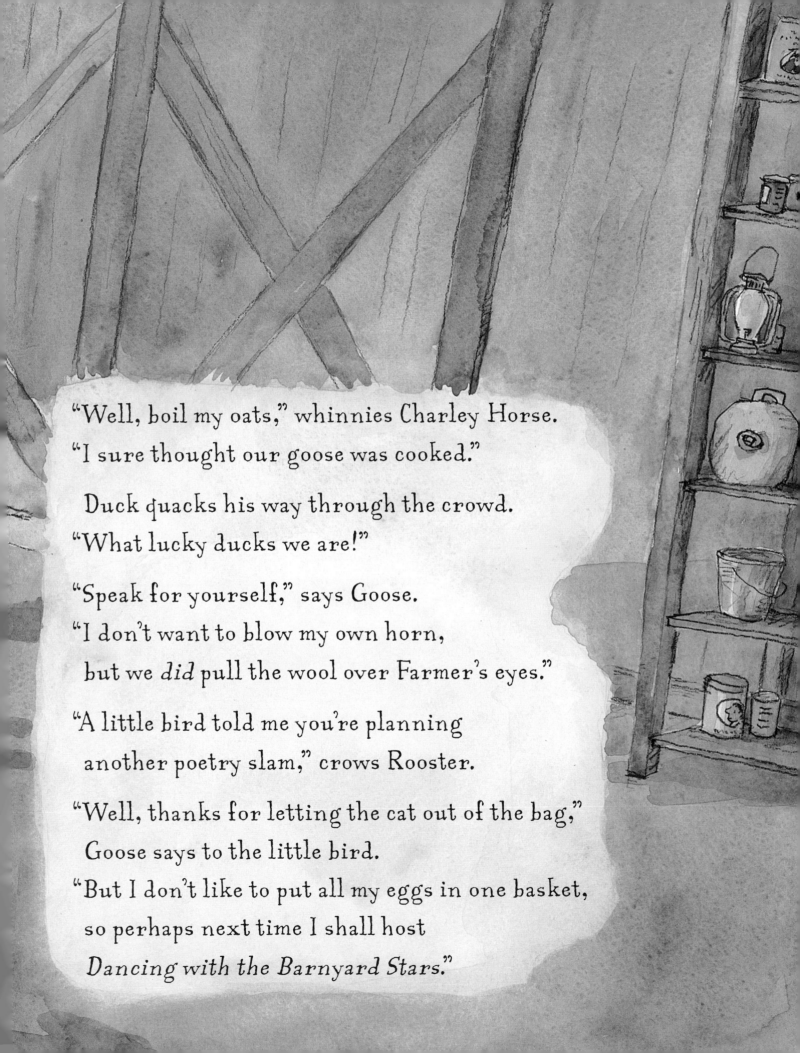

"Well, boil my oats," whinnies Charley Horse.
"I sure thought our goose was cooked."

Duck quacks his way through the crowd.
"What lucky ducks we are!"

"Speak for yourself," says Goose.
"I don't want to blow my own horn,
  but we *did* pull the wool over Farmer's eyes."

"A little bird told me you're planning
  another poetry slam," crows Rooster.

"Well, thanks for letting the cat out of the bag,"
  Goose says to the little bird.
"But I don't like to put all my eggs in one basket,
  so perhaps next time I shall host
  Dancing with the Barnyard Stars."

"And now, the talented Yo Mama Goose presents . . . *Swan Lake!*"